DROP DEAD

Babette Cole

RED FOX

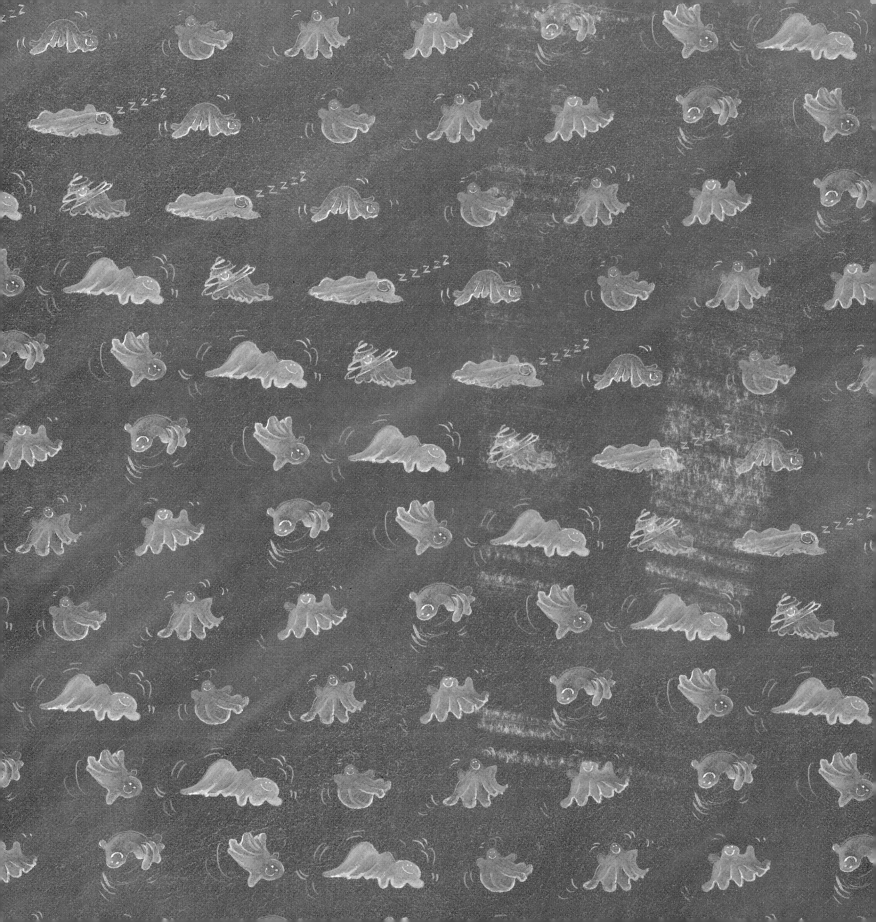

This book is dedicated to
my cat, Catsi, (1982 – 1996).
He is now what he
always wanted
to be...
a
Rottweiler!

"Gran and Grandad, why are you such bald old wrinklies?"

"We were bald wrinkly babies once!"

We learnt
dribbling and burping...

potty training,

and how to say simple words like

Poo Poo
and
Pee Pee

We learned
crawling,

standing on one leg,

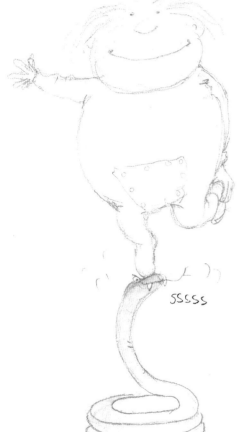

running and
jumping!

Then we went to school.

As we grew older we played different games.

At six years old.

At ten years old.

At sixteen years old.

When we were
teenagers we
experimented
with…

smoking…

driving Dad's car…

falling in love with the wrong person,

falling in love with the right person

and not being approved of.

We had college parties.

We failed to get jobs as scientists! So we went to work in films.

Grandad became   a stunt man!

Grandma became a famous film star!

We fell in love
and got married

on location!

We had your father – this was the only way
we could get him to bed.

When he grew up, he became a famous crocodile wrestler on the Nile.

There he met your mother

and they had you.

When we became grandparents we retired

and as we grew older
we became more
wrinkly.

Grandad has gone quite bald

We've got false teeth!

We forget things!

We've shrunk a bit...

but we still try
the odd stunt.

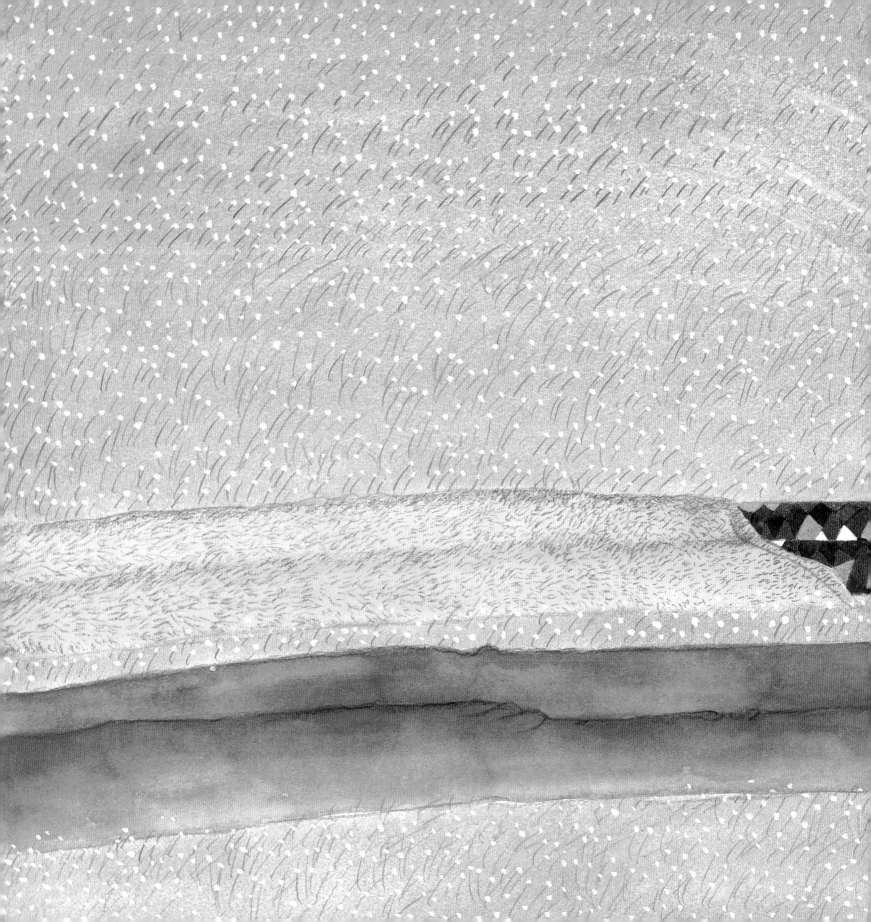

Even
though
we've
led
such
dangerous
lives,
one
day
we'll
just
drop
down
dead
like
everyone
else.

Then we might be recycled
as anything at all!

An octopus

a moose

a new baby

a worm

a sheep

a ghost

a pickled onion

an alien

or even two
scrawny
chickens.

What would you like us to be?

A Red Fox Book

Published by Random House Children's Books
20 Vauxhall Bridge Road, London SW1V 2SA

A division of Random House UK Ltd
London Melbourne Sydney Auckland
Johannesburg and agencies throughout the world

1 3 5 7 9 10 8 6 4 2

First published in Great Britain by Jonathan Cape 1996

Red Fox edition 1998

Printed in Singapore

RANDOM HOUSE UK Limited Reg. No. 954009

ISBN 0 09 965911 5

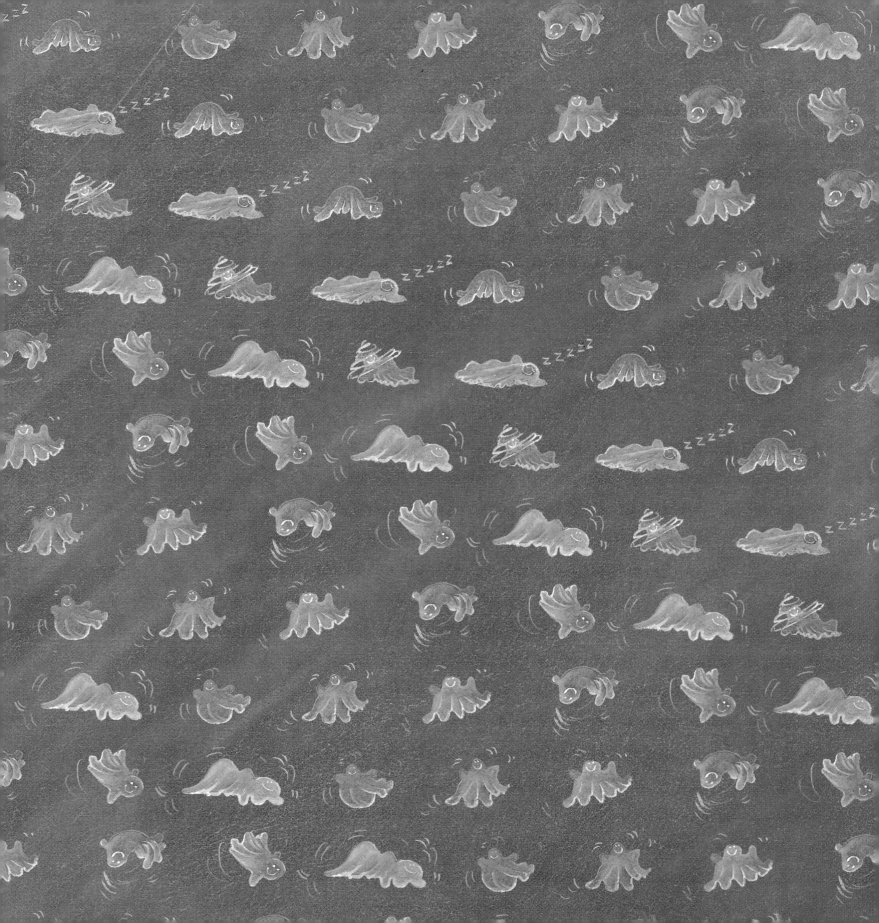

Picture Books by **Babette Cole** in Red Fox

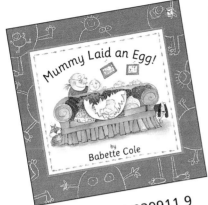

Mummy Laid an Egg!

Mum and Dad decide it's time they told the children about the facts of life...

'Brilliantly funny' SUNDAY TELEGRAPH

ISBN 0 09 929911 9

Feeling dizzy? Feeling sick? You need the expert attention of Doctor Dog!

'Charming, educative (in a rather naughty way) and funny… Take daily, repeatedly' OBSERVER

ISBN 0 09 965081 9

DROP DEAD

How we grew from one-year-old bald wrinklies into eighty-year-old bald wrinklies…

'Delightful… radical…' INDEPENDENT ON SUNDAY

ISBN 0 09 965911 5